CITIES AT WAR

LONDON
★ ★ ★

Michael Kronenwetter

New Discovery Books

New York

Maxwell Macmillan Canada
Toronto

Maxwell Macmillan International
New York   Oxford   Singapore   Sydney

PHOTOGRAPHIC ACKNOWLEDGMENTS
Front Cover: Magnum Photos, Inc. (George Rodger)
Back Cover: The Bettmann Archive
Interiors: The Bettmann Archive: 4, 7, 10, 13, 14, 16, 27, 37, 44, 46, 49, 50,
        55, 57, 59, 62, 66, 71, 74, 77, 79, 81, 82, 86, 91
        Magnum Photos, Inc.: (George Rodger) 20, 22, 25, 52, 61, 68, 75
        The Bettmann Archive/Hulton: 17, 18, 24, 26, 29, 31, 32, 34, 36,
        38, 40, 41, 42, 73, 84, 89

New Discovery Books
Macmillan Publishing Company
866 Third Avenue
New York, NY 10022

Maxwell Macmillan Canada, Inc.
1200 Eglinton Avenue East
Suite 200
Don Mills, Ontario M3C 3N1

Macmillan Publishing Company is part of the Maxwell Communication
Group of Companies.

First Edition

Printed in the United States of America

10 9 8 7 6 5 4 3 2 1

Library of Congress Cataloging-in-Publication Data
Kronenwetter, Michael.
        London / by Michael Kronenwetter.
            p.   cm. — (Cities at War)
        Includes bibliographical references.
        Summary: Examines the effects of World War II on the people of
London, with emphasis on the bombing raids and the evacuation of many
children to the surrounding countryside.
        ISBN 0-02-751050-6
        1. World War, 1939-1945—England—London—Juvenile literature.
2. London (England)—History—1800-1950—Juvenile literature.
[1. World War, 1939-1945—England—London. 2. London (England)—
History—1800-1950.]   I. Title. II. Series.
D760.8.L7K6 1992
942.1084—dc20   91-30306

CONTENTS

★ ★ ★

Schoolchildren in prewar London watch the opening of the magnificent London Tower Bridge, one of the city's most historic sites.

THE HEART OF THE EMPIRE

L ondon was the most important city in the world in 1939, the year World War II began. It was the world's biggest city, the capital of England, and the heart of one of the greatest empires the world had ever known.

England was a small island nation, smaller than the state of North Carolina. Yet, for centuries, the English had carried their civilization to the distant corners of the earth. In the process, little England had managed to acquire the most far-flung empire of any nation in history—the vast collection of lands and peoples known as the British Empire and Commonwealth. Roughly one-fifth of all the land area on Earth belonged to the British Empire, and the British navy ruled the seas.

Among the distant lands that owed allegiance to the British monarch were Canada, the largest country in North America; several colonies in Africa; a number of islands in the Caribbean; British

Guiana in South America; key coastal regions along the Persian Gulf, the Gulf of Aden, and the Red Sea; the huge subcontinent of India; and the entire continent of Australia.

And all these nations looked to London for leadership. King George VI and his queen, Elizabeth, made their official home at London's Buckingham Palace. The prime minister, the official who actually ran the British government, lived nearby at 10 Downing Street. The British Parliament—the oldest lawmaking body in the world—met in the huge Parliament buildings on the banks of the Thames River, in the Westminster borough of the city.

Wealth from around the empire flowed into the financial district known as The City. Many of the empire's brightest and most talented people flowed into London as well.

For people throughout Britain's many colonies and commonwealths, London was more than the heart of the empire, it was the heart of civilization itself. English was the world's most widely spoken language, and London's British Museum housed the finest library of books in English found anywhere. The same institution housed a priceless collection of archaeological treasures, brought to London from countries around the globe.

London was where Shakespeare had written his plays, where Dickens had written his novels, and where Karl Marx had written the Communist bible, *Das Kapital*. In 1939, it was home to some of the best symphony orchestras, ballet companies, and art museums in the world. The city's West End claimed to be the most active theater district anywhere. The University of London was the largest in England.

Historic buildings studded the city. Every British monarch since 1066 had been crowned in Westminster Abbey, and eighteen of them were buried beneath its roof. So were many other famous

Britons, including the first great English poet, Geoffrey Chaucer; the scientist and philosopher, Isaac Newton; and the naturalist, Charles Darwin. St. Paul's Cathedral stood where a Roman temple had rested in the seventh century; its own massive dome dated from the seventeenth. The Tower of London, once the home of kings and execution chamber of traitors, had been built in the eleventh. Scores of other London churches, homes, theaters, and taverns had stood on the same sites for centuries.

Buckingham Palace, the home of Britain's royal family

★ ★ ★

The 19th-century empire-builder Cecil Rhodes once told a young man to "remember that you are an Englishman, and have consequently won first prize in the lottery of life."[1] But not all the English were born equally lucky. The big winners in the lottery were those whose parents had a title or an enormous amount of money. They were the members of the upper class and could expect to be privileged and pampered all their lives.

The small winners were those whose fathers were successful businessmen or had a well-paying profession. (Very few women held well-paying jobs in 1939.) They were the middle class. They would have to work for a living or marry spouses who did. But, with a little luck and ability, their lives would be comfortable and rewarding.

Children whose parents had low-paying jobs or no jobs at all were the lottery's big losers. They were the lower class. That made

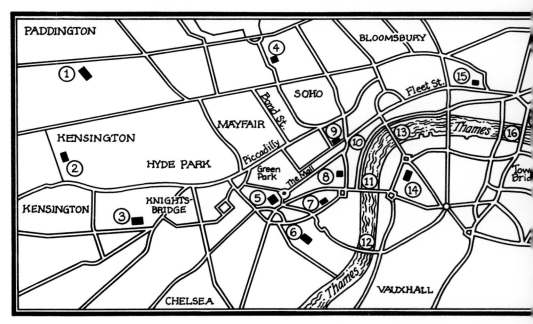

them part of the majority in prewar London, but it also put them at the bottom of the social heap.

For the children of the upper classes, London was a wonderland. It had real palaces, where real royalty lived, and exclusive toy shops, filled with the latest toys and games.

Upper-class children themselves lived in beautiful houses in lovely neighborhoods, like Mayfair or Bloomsbury, in the West End of the city. Outside, the air smelled green and fresh. Inside, everything smelled of furniture polish, fine cooking, and freshly washed linens.

They had servants to wait on them day and night. When they were infants, they had nannies to walk them to the park. When they got older, they had chauffeurs to drive them to school. As they grew up, there were horses to ride and an endless round of costume parties and dances to attend.

① Paddington Station
② Kensington Palace
③ Victoria and Albert Museum
④ Broadcasting House (B.B.C.)
⑤ Buckingham Palace
⑥ Westminster Cathedral
⑦ Westminster Abbey
⑧ 10 Downing Street
⑨ Trafalgar Square
⑩ Charing Cross Station
⑪ Westminster Bridge
⑫ Lambeth Bridge
⑬ Waterloo Bridge
⑭ Waterloo Station
⑮ St. Paul's Cathedral
⑯ London Bridge
⑰ Tower of London

Liverpool

ENGLAND

London

Petticoat Lane, a pushcart market in London's crowded East End

The one grim interruption in the easy pleasure of their lives was school. After elementary school, middle- and upper-class young men and some young women moved on to grammar schools. These were five-year institutions, similar to American high schools. The brightest and wealthiest boys were sent outside London to the so-called public schools like Rugby, Eton, and Harrow. These were really very expensive private boarding schools. Classes were hard, and discipline was strict. Even a prince's son might be whipped if he misbehaved.

School could be hard, but summer holidays made up for it. There would be trips to the family's country estate, or voyages abroad. For those with adventurous parents, there were excursions to exotic places like India, where they would ride elephants and be entertained in the palaces of Indian princes. For the rest, there would be trips to the Continent, where upper-class English families basked in the gilded luxuries of Rome and Paris, and bathed in the sunshine of the French Riviera.

For the children of the poor, however, there were no servants, no luxuries, and very little sun. Life had always been hard for the poor, but in 1939 there were more of them than there had been before. The 1930s had been a decade of economic depression, and hundreds of thousands of Londoners were out of work.

Millions of Londoners lived in tiny apartments in rickety firetrap buildings in London's East End. Ten people were often crowded into a single room. Many families didn't own enough chairs for everyone to sit down at the same time. At night, there was hardly room for everyone to lie down to sleep, even on the floor. Those lucky enough to share a bed with two or three family members had no room to roll over. There was no running water. One filthy toilet had to be shared by every family on the floor. There was no sanitation, and the air inside the tenements stank of garbage and human waste. Going outside gave little relief, for the air in the streets was thick with poisonous smoke from nearby factories.

For these children, education stopped after the lower grades. To get more, parents had to pay, and there was no money. The law required children to stay in school till they were 14, but many left before that. They had to. They needed to work in order to survive.

Most people were trapped in the social class they were born in for their entire lives. Some unlucky members of the middle class would suffer financial disaster and fall into the lower class. It was even possible (though unlikely) for a member of the middle class to rise into the upper class: if a man were extraordinarily successful at business, or if a woman married well. But it was almost impossible for a poor man or woman to move up out of the lower class.

Upper-class children could look forward to being the nation's leaders, and the rulers of the empire. Middle-class children could hope to be comfortable, perhaps even prosperous. But the children of the lower class had nothing to look forward to except the same poverty in which they were raised.

So, although they all lived in London, the children of the different classes might have been in different worlds. Their lives had little in common. But that was about to change. Before 1939 was over, Britain would be at war. England would be threatened with invasion by the most powerful military machine in Europe. Everyone in the country—rich and poor, young and old—would share the same deadly dangers. And the children of every social class would be facing death from the skies, and the possible destruction of the city they all called home.

Nothing would ever be the same again.

Piccadilly Circus bustles with activity.

A late-breaking headline announces Britain's entrance into the war.

★ ★ ★ ★ ★ ★ ★ ★ ★ ★

2

"THIS COUNTRY IS AT WAR"

The war that threatened to destroy England was started by the Nazi government of Germany and its leader, Adolf Hitler. The Nazis dreamed of conquering Europe. Although a treaty limited Germany to a small military, they built the most modern and powerful army and navy in Europe—and, in fact, the world.

German troops crossed into Austria on March 12, 1938, and Hitler announced *Anschluss,* or union, between Germany and Austria. Hitler then demanded a part of Czechoslovakia called the Sudetenland. It seemed that he was determined to gobble up his neighbors until someone forced him to stop. Europe seemed to be slipping rapidly toward war.

Some Britons warned that if Hitler wasn't stopped soon, the Nazis would march across Europe. England would be isolated and helpless. It was better to fight now, they thought, than to wait till

Chamberlain and Hitler meet at the Munich Conference.

Britain had no allies left in Europe. Others sympathized with Germany. Some even admired Hitler. If war came to Europe, they wanted Britain to stay out of it.

Britain's prime minister, Neville Chamberlain, also wanted Britain to stay out of war, but not because he was sympathetic to Hitler. He hated the Nazis and opposed Hitler's efforts to expand Germany, but he knew that Britain's military was not ready for war. It was certainly no match for Hitler's huge new war machine.

In the fall of 1938, Chamberlain flew to Munich, Germany, to meet with Hitler and two other European leaders. On September

Chamberlain and his wife wave to cheering crowds celebrating the signing of the Munich Pact.

30, they signed an agreement known as the Munich Pact. It gave the Sudetenland to Germany in return for Hitler's promise that he was satisfied.

Back home in England, Chamberlain proudly announced the end of any threat of war. The Munich Pact, he declared, meant "peace for our time." He was greeted as a hero by a large crowd waiting at 10 Downing Street. As he made his way through the crowd, women cried out their thanks to him. Tears of joy were streaming down their faces.

Not everyone was so happy, however. An angry member of

Winston Churchill (right) correctly predicted Britain's entry into World War II.

the British Parliament named Winston Churchill bitterly attacked the Munich Pact. England, he said, had faced a choice between war and shame. "She has chosen shame," he declared bitterly. "And will get war."[1]

He was right.

Less than six months later, the German army marched out of the Sudetenland and took control of all of Czechoslovakia. The Munich Pact was dead. When Hitler then demanded Poland, even Chamberlain realized that the Nazis would not be stopped by appeasement. If Poland was attacked, he warned Germany, Britain would fight. There would be war.

At dawn, on Friday, September 1, 1939, German troops stormed into Poland. That same day, German planes began bombing the Polish capital city, Warsaw.

In those days before television was available, people turned to the radio when great events were taking place. All that weekend, the people of England stayed near their radios, frightened but eager to hear what would happen next. What would England do?

At 11:00 in the morning of Sunday, September 3, they heard the anguished voice of their prime minister. "I have to tell you," he announced, "that ... this country is at war with Germany."[2]

At 6:00 that evening, the English gathered around their radios again. This time, it was to hear the voice of their king, George VI. George had a stutter that he'd worked very hard to overcome, so he always spoke slowly and with great care. But now, speaking the most solemn words he would ever have to say, his voice was firm and steady.

"War can no longer be confined to the battlefield," he said, speaking especially to the people of London and other cities that probably would be bombed. "But for the sake of all that we ourselves hold dear, and of the world's order and peace, it is unthinkable that we should refuse to meet the challenge.... To this high purpose I now call my people at home and my peoples across the seas.... If one and all we keep resolutely faithful to it, and ready for whatever service or sacrifice it may demand, then with God's help, we shall prevail."[3]

★ ★ ★

British schoolboys wait to board a train during the evacuations.

★ ★ ★ ★ ★ ★ ★ ★ ★

3

AN ENFORCED VACATION

Minutes after Chamberlain's announcement that war had begun, air-raid sirens screamed over the city. Every Londoner's stomach churned with alarm. They all knew what the bombing of London could mean. Besides the explosions, there would be terrible fires and, perhaps, the unknown horrors of gas. Military experts had warned there could be as many as 100,000 casualties in one week. The city might well be smashed to rubble within two weeks. Everyone knew it was bound to happen sometime, but no one had expected it so *soon*.

Even so, there was no panic. London had been preparing for war for a long time. Most residents—including the king and queen—simply rushed to the nearest air-raid shelter. But not everyone.

Many people dashed to their windows, others ran outside, and some even climbed to their rooftops. All over London, children slipped from their worried parents' grasps and scrambled out to get

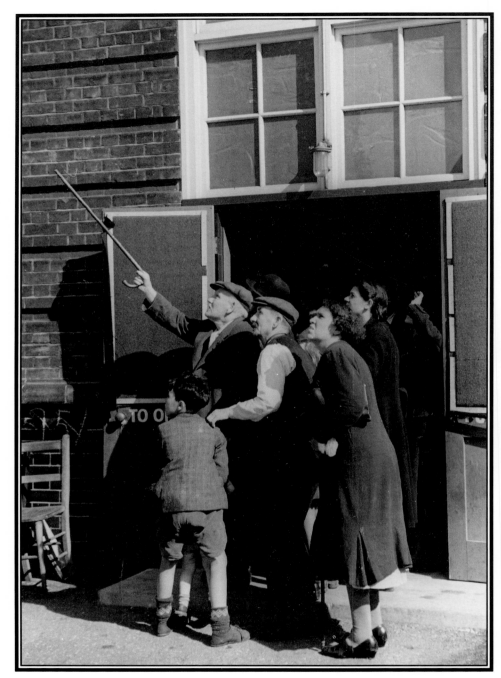

Londoners scan the skies for signs of German bombers.

a better view. Their hearts thumping in their chests, they scanned the skies, hoping for a glimpse of the first air battle of the war. But there was nothing to see except the blue sky and sunshine of an incredibly beautiful summer day. The sirens had been a false alarm.

It was an omen of things to come. The sirens would wail over London many times that winter, but no bombers would appear. Little would happen anywhere. Over 200,000 British troops, known as the British Expeditionary Force (BEF), quickly sailed to France to help defend England's ally against a possible German invasion. But the invasion never came. There were some air skirmishes over the British coast, and some ships were torpedoed at sea, but no great battles took place anywhere—on land, on the sea, or in the air. It came to be known as the "phony war."

Everyone knew the phony war couldn't last forever. The real war was bound to begin soon. Like some beast in the jungle, it was only licking its chops, toying with its victims before it devoured them.

★　★　★

Even before Chamberlain's announcement, the lives of London's children had already been disrupted by the coming war. Despite the fact that they were still on summer vacations, all children had been ordered to report to their schools in late August. There, they were told that war might start at any moment and that the city was almost certain to be bombed. In order to protect them, they were to be evacuated—sent out of the city—until the danger passed.

The next few days were hard ones for London's families. Evacuation was strongly encouraged, but it was voluntary. Each family had to decide whether to keep its children in the city or send them away. It was a heartbreaking decision. In the end, most left, but many thousands stayed behind.

No one knew how long the ones who left would be away. It could be weeks, or months, or even years. Some might never return to their homes and families again. Some might have no homes or families left to return to.

Children were allowed one small suitcase, along with the clothes they could wear, carry, and jam into their pockets. Many mothers broke into tears as they packed their child's toothbrush,

A little boy clutches tightly to his parcel of belongings as his soldier father kisses him good-bye.

As the threat of war grew, more Londoners were evacuated to the English countryside.

A train full of London schoolchildren leaves Blackhouse Road Station.

soap, and comb, and one change of underwear.

On September 1, hundreds of thousands of young Londoners walked out of their homes on the way to the unknown. Some of the older ones kissed their mothers good-bye at the door and struck out bravely on their own. Most of the younger ones were taken to their schools or to an assigned train or bus station by their mothers. There were few fathers at the departure points. Most of them had to be at work.

Mothers would accompany some of the infants and smaller children, but most would be going alone. Except for those who had country relatives willing to take them in, they would be farmed out to strangers all over rural England. Not even their parents would know where they were going until after they had arrived.

The younger children had pieces of paper pinned to their clothes with their names on them. At the assembly points, each evacuee was given a little bag with cans of corned beef and condensed milk, so they wouldn't arrive on their host's doorstep hungry and demanding food. Many children carried pictures of their parents in their pockets. Some clutched their favorite doll or blanket.

Some of the children were eager and excited. They were looking forward to a vacation, a trip to the country, where most of them had never been. But most were just confused and scared.

Those huddled together at the train stations were also extremely uncomfortable. Although it was very hot, they had been ordered to wear their winter coats. They milled about on the platforms, sweating under layers of clothes and inhaling the foul smells made by the trains. Mothers and children alike grew faint from the heat, the tension, and the looming sense of loss.

Eventually, the train or bus arrived. Last hugs were given. Last "goodbye luv"s were said. Then the children were packed into the vehicles. Faces were pressed against windows. Eyes searched desperately for one last glimpse of Mother. Then they were gone.

✯ ✯ ✯

In three short days, one million children were plucked from their homes in England's cities and distributed to other people's houses throughout the English countryside. The prime minister called it "the greatest social experiment which England has ever undertaken."[1]

There was an effort to keep children from the same family together. Some whole schools were evacuated to the same country village. But many youngsters found themselves alone in places as unfamiliar to them as a foreign country. Many had never been away from their families before, not even for a night. Some had never set foot outside London.

The country people had been ordered to take the children in, and many resented it. Others saw the older children only as servants, extra hands to do the household chores or the heavy work around the farm.

Even the most well-meaning country people were often shocked by the condition of the children who showed up on their doorsteps. Many who came from the London slums were filthy and badly clothed. Tens of thousands were sickly, undernourished, and covered with lice and fleas. One community was so alarmed by the vermin that they fumigated the local school after a reception for the children there. Some of the poorest children had no sense of hygiene at all. Outraged hosts reported that they relieved themselves on the bedroom floor.

Respectable country people were even more shocked by their guests' rowdy behavior. "We have to keep on the lookout the whole time," one farm wife told a visitor. "Those children will chase the

A nursery school class practices carrying their gas masks to a shelter during a bomb drill.

hens, the sheep, and even the heifers.... They will break anything.... They have that big garden, but they play only in the road." And the country people knew just whom to blame. "Their mothers have no control over them, and don't seem to care whether the children obey or not, or how dirty they are."[2]

The authorities had assumed that sending along the children's mothers over would make the children's adjustment easier, but instead they often made things worse. They clashed with their hosts over everything from how to punish the children to how to cook the stew. The government finally decided that it was better for the mothers to stay at home.

At first, the children were as shocked by the country as the country was by them. "The country is a funny place," one reported. "They never tell you you can't have no more to eat, and [the space] under the bed is wasted."[3] A 13-year-old boy wrote that his little sister Rose was so bewildered she "whispered for days. Everything was so clean in the room. We were even given flannels and tooth-brushes. We'd never cleaned our teeth up till then. And hot water came from the tap. And there was a lavatory upstairs...and clean sheets. This was all very odd. And rather scaring."[4]

Many city children quickly came to love the country life. The plentiful food, the comfortable beds—and even cleanliness—were very appealing. After the grime and the crowds of the city, they gloried in the freshness of the country air and the freedom of the open spaces. The weather was beautiful in England that fall, and they delighted in walking through the woods and fields, spotting wild badgers, pheasants, beavers, and a host of other creatures they had never seen before.

For other children, however, life in the country was a night-mare. Homesickness overcame them. Night after night they cried

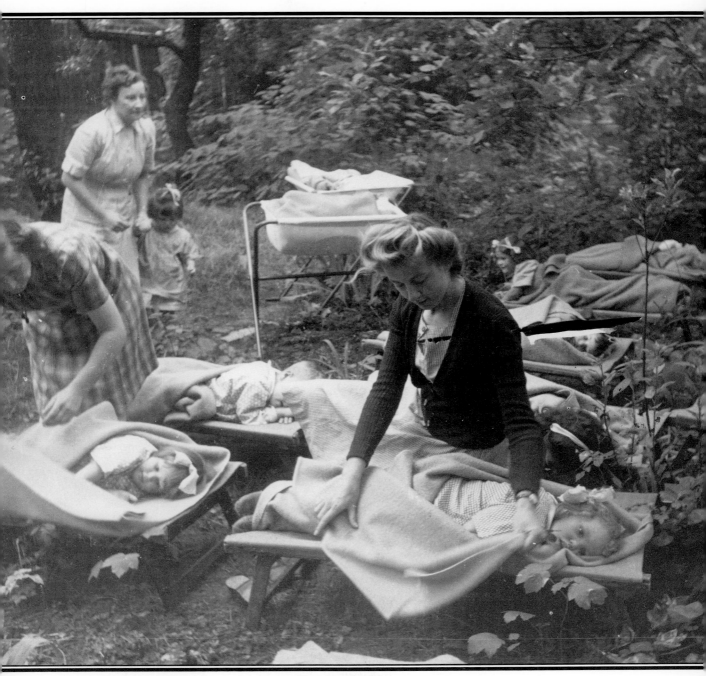

A country garden becomes a leafy bedroom for evacuated London children.

Evacuated children rush to be reunited with their parents during a visit arranged by the British railroad.

themselves to sleep. Bed-wetting was a constant problem. In their hearts, they blamed themselves for the separation from their families.

Others just didn't like the country. They were bored by the slow pace of country life, and frightened by the animals. They longed for the bustle and excitement of London—bombs or no bombs.

And there were no bombs.

Even after winter had settled over England, nothing fell on the city but snow. Tens of thousands of homesick children pleaded to return. Parents began to wonder whether it was worth the pain of separation to keep them in the country. As the weeks passed, more and more children made their way back to the cities. By November, 20,000 of them had already returned to London.

The government appealed to parents to keep their children safe in the countryside. As Christmas approached, social workers staged Christmas plays in villages all over England. "Once a child gets a part in a play," one explained, "he will refuse to go home for Christmas."[5]

But many went home anyway.

The signs of war: a blackout notice is posted on a London streetlight.

4

PREPARING FOR THE WORST

When the children returned to the city, it looked very different. Antiaircraft (ack-ack) guns sprouted on rooftops and on the lawns of London's beautiful parks. Still more ack-ack guns could be seen rolling through the streets on the backs of trucks, ready to race to wherever the danger came.

The lower walls of buildings were hidden behind piles of sandbags, packed snugly to cushion the force of exploding bombs. The windows of stores, offices, and homes were crisscrossed with tape. An untaped window could shatter from a distant bomb blast and send daggers of glass tearing through the rooms inside. Some patriotic homeowners, like the parents of the British writer and actor Peter Ustinov, arranged the tape in the pattern of the British union jack.

Street and highway signs had been taken down to make it hard for German invaders to tell where they were. But there was lit-

A British woman buys blackout material to cover her windows.

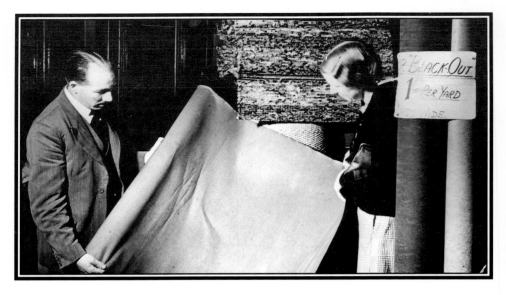

tle hope of that. Nothing could be done to hide London's many well-known landmarks—Big Ben, Tower Bridge, Buckingham Palace, and scores of others. All an invader would need was a good tourist map.

At night, London was a city of shadows in the darkness. Strict blackout rules were in effect. People were ordered to pull black curtains over all windows to keep light from showing. Streetlights were almost entirely covered over, and so were the windows of trains and other public vehicles. Any light visible from the air would make it easier for the pilots of night bombers to tell where their targets were.

There seemed to be more women and fewer men on London's streets. Uniforms were everywhere, and not just worn by men. The crisp-looking young women of the WATS (Women's Auxiliary Territorial Service), the WAFS (Women's Auxiliary Air Force), and the WAVS (Women's Auxiliary Volunteer Service) each had distinctive costumes of their own.

*Members of the
Women's
Auxiliary Air
Force suited up
for duty.*

The changed face of London: a woman waits in front of a public shelter.

Able-bodied young men were hard to find. Hundreds of thousands of them had been whisked out of London for military service. Most had been sent to military posts around the country, while others had been shipped across the English Channel to join the BEF in France. Many would never return to London alive.

While many people were leaving the city, others were arriving. Almost all the newcomers were foreigners. Most were military men: French, Canadians, Australians, and others who had come to help the mother country fight its war. Others were refugees: Jews, Poles, Czechs, Austrians, and other Europeans, fleeing from the path of the Nazi steamroller.

Overall, though, London's population was shrinking. By January 1940, there were roughly three million fewer adults living in London than when the war began. London was no longer the most populated city in the world.

★ ★ ★

Many children returned home to find their beloved pets dead. Hundreds of thousands of worried owners had already had their dogs, cats, and caged birds destroyed for fear they would suffer during the air raids.

All the poisonous snakes in the London Zoo had also been killed in the early days of the war. Authorities feared that a bomb might set the deadly serpents loose in the city. As the war went on and food shortages developed, many more pets and zoo animals were "put down" to keep them from starving. Others had to change their diets. Sea lions in the zoo were tossed pieces of cheap meat doused in cod liver oil to convince them that they were swallowing fish.

★ ★ ★

Every Londoner had received a gas mask during the first war scare

*Gas-masked
Londoners in
a shelter*

in 1938. Now they carried the masks with them everywhere they went, even on trips to the corner pub. There were full-size masks for adults, smaller ones for children, and special masks for infants that were almost as big as they were. Stores even sold models designed for pets. At home, people kept blankets handy, to stuff under doors to keep out gas.

There were hundreds of public air-raid shelters all over the

A family practices getting into their backyard shelter.

city. Most were located underground, in the basements of large buildings, or in the deepest stations of the tube, the London subway system. Several were located in churches. In some poor neighborhoods, where there were few strong buildings, people were told to take what shelter they could under the arches of the city's above-ground railroad system. In addition, thousands of portable air-raid shelters had been distributed to householders. Some were like small

41

sheds, made out of corrugated iron. Others were more like iron igloos, partly buried in the ground.

★   ★   ★

Winston Churchill reviews a group of Home Guard volunteers.

Winter turned to spring, and still the Germans did not attack. People began to wonder whether they ever would. Maybe the whole thing had been a bluff. On April 5, 1940, Prime Minister Chamberlain held a meeting and said that Hitler had "missed the bus." The time for him to strike was past.

Four days later, Hitler struck.

German troops invaded Denmark and Norway. The phony war was over. The real war had begun.

On May 10, German troops invaded France, as well as the Netherlands, Belgium, and Luxembourg. That same day, Neville Chamberlain left 10 Downing Street in disgrace. He was replaced as prime minister by Sir Winston Churchill, who had been serving as head of the British navy.

Churchill was a round, chubby man who walked with a cane and smoked big, smelly cigars. He had a red bulb of a nose, and people said he drank too much. He looked more like a beardless Santa Claus than a warrior, but he would prove to be an inspiration to the people of England.

Chamberlain had done everything he could to avoid war; Churchill almost seemed to welcome it. "I have nothing to offer," he told a worried nation, "but blood, toil, tears, and sweat."[1] The words were frightening, but his voice was confident. He spoke in a cross between a purr and a growl and seemed to delight in the words he used. He spoke with such fierce determination that people believed him when he promised them "victory, however long and hard the road may be."[2]

It was soon clear that the road would be very long and very hard indeed. The German troops rolled over France. Within two weeks, the BEF was trapped with its back to the sea near the French town of Dunkirk. On May 26, more than 360,000 helpless British

A British transport ship brings soldiers home from Dunkirk as part of Operation Dynamo.

and French troops began fleeing back across the Channel to England. A massive rescue operation, code-named Operation Dynamo, was launched to save them.

Almost 30,000 of the Allied soldiers were killed, wounded, or captured, but over 200,000 British soldiers and nearly 140,000 French soldiers escaped. Operation Dynamo was the biggest British military operation of the war so far. Churchill called it a miracle, but it was still a retreat. The German army was now only 21 miles away across the Channel. The situation seemed hopeless, but Churchill was determined not to give up.

"We shall fight on the seas and oceans," he promised grimly. "We shall fight, with growing confidence, and growing strength in the air. We shall defend our island, whatever the cost shall be. We shall fight on the beaches, we shall fight on the landing grounds, we shall fight in the fields and in the streets, we shall fight in the hills; we shall never surrender."[3]

"The Battle of France is over," he declared. "The Battle of Britain is about to begin.... Hitler knows he must break us in this island or lose the war.... If we fail, the whole world, including the United States, and all that we have known and cared for, will sink into the abyss of a new dark age.... Let us therefore brace ourselves to our duty and so bear ourselves that if the British Commonwealth and Empire last for a thousand years, men will still say, 'This was their finest hour.' "[4]

Firemen fight one of the fires that ravaged the docks in the East End at the start of the Blitz.

THE BLITZ

September 7, 1940, was a beautiful day, much like the one a year before when war had been declared. People would look back on this day and marvel at how blue the sky had been, how incredible it was that such terrible events could take place on such a lovely day.

One of those who would remember was a 14-year-old girl named Jane Hartwright. Jane had been evacuated the year before and hated it. Now she was glad to be back with her family in their home on the outskirts of London. She was out in the yard that Saturday afternoon, standing in the family garden. Fifty years later, Jane vividly remembers the beauty—and the horror—of that day.

"We were watching what we thought were our own bombers. The sky was *littered* with formations of bombers—wave after wave after wave. We couldn't see the markings. They were too high. And everybody thought, Oh marvelous, look at this! It's like an air display. It went on and on, and then we heard distant noises...."[1]

It wasn't British bombers they were seeing. And it was no air display. Seven miles away, the same planes passing over Jane's garden were dropping deadly cargoes on the London docks. The Blitz—the long expected air attack on London—had begun.

More than 300 German bombers took part in that first raid, protected by more than twice that many fighter planes. Before they were done, warehouses, factories, and miles of docks were in ruins, and more than a thousand fires were raging in London. The worst damage was in the poor neighborhoods surrounding the docks. In places like Limehouse and Silverton, whole blocks were turned into rubble.

Terrified people scurried through the streets. Frantic parents searched for missing children, while children whose parents had been killed wandered aimlessly. Whole families pushed their treasured belongings in front of them in baby carriages, rushing to escape the inferno their neighborhoods had become. Most were going nowhere in particular, only as far as they could get from the sudden horror that had engulfed them. The strongest walkers managed to make it all the way out of the city. They slept in country fields that night, surrounded by the distant rumble of the bombs raining down on London.

After a few hours, the sun went down. Most of England fell into darkness, but near the docks of London it stayed light all night long. People swore that you could read a book by the light of those fires.

Even seven miles away, reflected flames made the windows of the Hartwright house glow orange in the darkness. "It was horrific," Jane says now. "We hardly moved from our gardens. We were

The effects of a German bombing raid

A barrage balloon floats over Tower Bridge

just paralyzed, you know. I think we stayed up most of the night, just watching. And it didn't stop."[2]

It wouldn't stop—it hardly even paused—for 57 days.

★ ★ ★

On July 15, 1940, Hitler had issued the secret order to invade England. The invasion was code-named Operation Sea Lion and scheduled for September. Before it could take place, however, the Germans needed air supremacy—control of the skies over England. With it, the invasion was sure to succeed, because the Germans had overwhelming power on the ground. But without it, the invasion would fail. The Royal Air Force (RAF) could destroy any invading force as it tried to come ashore.

For the next several weeks, the *Luftwaffe* (German air force) concentrated its attacks on RAF planes and air bases. There were few raids on English cities and none at all on London. Hitler did not want to give Britain a reason for bombing German cities. Besides, the cities were not important. It was the RAF the Germans had to worry about.

Then, in late August, a German bomber had dropped a few bombs on London. It was probably a mistake, but the British government responded with a series of bombing raids against Berlin. Hitler was outraged. He ordered the Luftwaffe to forget about the RAF bases and attack England's cities—particularly London.

For a solid week, London endured the almost constant pounding of German bombs. After a year of phony war, the massive attack seemed to take the British defenses by surprise.

London relied on three major defense systems. The first was a network of huge, silver-gray barrage balloons that rimmed the city. Ann Ackermann, who was a little girl in 1940, remembers them as giant Dumbos floating in the sky.[3] The balloons were held to the

Children watch as German planes fly over their neighborhood.

ground by steel cables that were intended to act as obstacles to bombers flying low over the city. In those first days, however, the cables were not long enough to cause the attackers much trouble. By forcing the bombers to fly a little higher, they only made it harder for the British ack-ack guns to shoot them down; and by throwing off the bombardiers' aim, they made it more likely that a bomb aimed at a warehouse might hit an apartment building instead.

Even the RAF was little use at first. It was reeling from weeks of intense Luftwaffe attacks. In the first week of the Blitz, the RAF only managed to shoot down 225 planes, while losing 185 from its own much smaller force.

But that week was vital to the RAF. While the Germans concentrated their attacks on the cities, they left the battered RAF bases alone. That gave the RAF time to recover its strength. Injured pilots had time to heal, overworked mechanics had time to repair damaged planes, and fresh supplies and reinforcements had time to arrive.

On September 15, the Luftwaffe launched a massive raid on London. It wasn't as big as the first raid, but London was already badly damaged and its defenders were tired. Hitler hoped this would be the knockout, the blow that won the battle—and, perhaps, the war. By then, however, the RAF was ready. Hundreds of British Spitfire and Hurricane fighters vaulted into the air to battle the attackers. The action was fierce. There were 200 dogfights—one-on-one battles between planes—in the first half hour alone. Much of the fighting took place in the skies over London itself.

Some of the most daring children ran outside to watch the dogfighters locked in mortal combat overhead. All that could be seen clearly from the ground were the white trails left by the exhausts of the planes' engines. From that distance, the planes seemed to move almost lazily, skywriting crazy patterns in the blueness of the sky.

It was the largest air battle that had ever taken place. When it was over, the British claimed a great victory. London newspapers boasted that the RAF had shot down seven planes for every one they had lost. That was a great exaggeration, but the Luftwaffe had failed in its attempt to take control of the skies over London.

Operation Sea Lion was postponed. It would never be rescheduled.

★ ★ ★

The Blitz brought about a second evacuation of children from London. Once again, hundreds of thousands of young people were rapidly dispatched around the countryside. Once again, hundreds of thousands more stayed behind.

London's schools had been closed during most of the first evacuation. Many of the school buildings had been commandeered for military or civil defense purposes. By April 1940, however, all students had been ordered back to school, at least part-time. Now the Blitz closed many of the schools again, but some stayed open throughout the bombings.

With many fathers away at war, and many mothers doing volunteer work, the children were left unsupervised most of the time. Lord De La Warr, the head of Britain's Board of Education, announced that 400,000 children were getting "no schooling or care at all."[4] Instead, he complained, they were running wild in the streets of London. "Some children in the East End are going to bed at midnight and rising at noon," one welfare officer explained. "One magistrate has commented to me that we are encouraging a generation of Artful Dodgers."[5] (The Artful Dodger is a child pickpocket in Charles Dickens's *Oliver Twist*.)

A doubledecker bus blown over by the force of an explosion.

The roaming bands often turned to vandalism. With so much destruction all around, it hardly seemed to matter. Things got so bad that the Air Raid Precautions Service began locking public air-raid shelters between bombings to protect them from the young looters.

★ ★ ★

The Blitz continued through the winter and into the spring. Besides ordinary bombs, the Germans used large land mines, packed with explosives, that drifted to the ground on parachutes. When they reached the ground they exploded with terrific force, often destroying several small buildings at once.

Some bombs didn't go off right away. Falling through the roofs of empty buildings or onto schoolyards, they became giant booby traps, exploding later, after people had returned to their normal activities.

German fighters would sometimes swoop down to machine-gun pedestrians trapped out in the open. They flew so low that a woman, who looked out her front window to see a plane machine-gunning a school building across the street, could see the pilot's face. Fortunately no children were hit, but a young nurse walking in the street was killed.

The bombers pounded the city so constantly that air-raid sirens, bombs, and all-clear signals tumbled after each other in confusing patterns. When there was finally a moment of silence, people couldn't remember whether the all-clear had sounded or not.

Once the RAF got better at shooting down daylight attackers, the Luftwaffe changed tactics. By mid-October, the bombers were coming almost entirely at night. Some nights, the raids went on without stop from sundown till sunrise.

Londoners were grateful for the air-raid sirens, but they hat-

A rescue crew searches for people trapped by an explosion.

ed the shrieking sound they made. Music experts pointed out that this was the tritone—a musical chord that had once been called "the devil in music." People complained so much about the ugly noise that the government cut the time they wailed from two minutes to one. As loud as they were, not everyone could hear the sirens. One deaf woman slept with a string tied to her toe and hanging out the window. Whenever the sirens sounded, the local air-raid warden came by and gave it a yank to wake her up.

Hurrying through the blacked-out streets, people could sometimes hear another sound: the distant hum of German planes approaching the city. As the attackers drew closer, the drone became a growl. Soon it was joined by the bursts of the city's ack-ack guns and finally by the deafening blasts of the bombs themselves. During the heaviest raids, all these sounds melded into a single noise, like the roar of a great thunderstorm rolling across the sky.

With the city blacked out below, the German pilots needed light to see their targets. For this reason, the Germans prayed for clear weather, while the Londoners prayed for rain and fog. The Thames River was a great help to the attackers. Flowing to London from the sea, it reflected the light from the moon and stars like a silver arrow pointing straight to the heart of the city.

Eventually, the Germans provided their own light by dropping bombs specially designed to start fires. These incendiary bombs set off blazes that lit up the city for blocks around, often showing the bombers their targets for nights to come.

★ ★ ★

The bombs spared nothing. Homes were hit. Apartment buildings. Schools. Nurseries. Hospitals. Historic monuments. At first, the East End area near the docks suffered most of the damage. As always, it seemed to some of the poor residents that the lower classes were being asked to suffer while the upper classes remained safe and protected.

By November, however, the Germans were pummeling the wealthier sections of the city as well. The House of Lords, the home of the Archbishop of Canterbury, and Westminster Abbey were all hit on the same day. Forty members of Parliament were almost killed when a bomb struck the exclusive Carlton Club while they were dining there. A section of the 8-foot-thick wall of the Tower of

London burns as the Germans hold a night raid.

London was smashed to pieces. Even the altar of the king's private chapel in Buckingham Palace was destroyed by a bomb. An old family bible that had belonged to Queen Victoria was found among the debris.

According to reporter James Minifie, the Germans had made a terrible mistake. "Had [they] continued to concentrate on the East End they might have created a class conflict. By bombing London indiscriminately they killed their chances of doing such a thing and united the city's population as never before."[6]

People were surprised to find that the explosions often sucked the air toward them, rather than blasting it away. An 18-year-old boy named Len Jones later reported that the suction from a nearby blast was so strong it ripped his shirt, and he could feel his eyeballs being sucked out of his head.[7]

Horrors were everywhere. Children woke up in the morning to find that their parents had been killed during the night. A man left home to go to the cinema, telling his wife and children to wait for him in a nearby shelter. When he returned, he found his home in ruins and his whole family dead. A bomb had hit before they had had a chance to leave the house. A young woman doing duty as an air-raid warden came upon the head of a friend lying in a public park.

✶ ✶ ✶

That winter the Germans changed tactics again, launching massive incendiary attacks that seemed intended to burn London to the ground. In a single night, the Germans dropped 70,000 incendiary bombs on the city.

In an effort to spot the fires early, and so have some chance of putting them out, thousands of men and women were pressed into service as fire-watchers. "Hitherto," Churchill would write,

Londoners scan a list of people killed during the raids for the names of friends and family.

The dome of St. Paul's Cathedral rises above the black smoke of the Blitz.

"we had encouraged the Londoners to take cover.... But now, 'To the basements' must be replaced with 'To the roofs.' " Even while the enemy bombers roared over the city spewing their deadly fire, these ordinary citizens stood watch on their rooftops, exposing themselves to incredible danger. Thanks to them, Churchill wrote, "thousands of fires were extinguished before they took hold."[8] Unfortunately, however, thousands of others raged out of control.

One of the worst incendiary raids came on December 29, 1940. One hundred thirty German planes soared over the city that night, spreading fire in their wake. Before it was over, the entire area around St. Paul's Cathedral was ablaze. Great flames ravaged the city, lighting up the streets for a mile around, while deadly black smoke choked the air. Survivors would later refer to it as the second Great Fire of London. The first Great Fire, in 1666, started in a bakery, and destroyed many buildings as it burned for five days.

Between 1,500 and 2,000 separate fires raged in London that night. The flames jumped from building to building, street to street. They roamed the city like hungry beasts, coming together to devour whole blocks, and even whole neighborhoods. In desperation, fire fighters blew up undamaged buildings to open up spaces the fires could not cross.

The raid had been timed for a night when the Thames River was at its lowest. This meant that the water pressure in London was low to begin with. Under the increased demand from thousands of fire hoses, it dropped to almost nothing. Desperate fire fighters strung hoses out to the center of the river to draw water from as great a depth as possible. Even so, they could do little. The strongest jet of water was not equal to the oceans of flame. By the time the fires were put out—or burned themselves out—the men and women of the fire services were exhausted. It might have been even worse if bad weather hadn't forced the Germans to return home after only a few hours.

The next day, the city's residents climbed out of the shelters to examine the wreckage. Whole neighborhoods were in ruins. St. Paul's Cathedral had survived, but everything around it was smoldering rubble. Useless fire hoses lay tangled in the streets like nests of huge dead snakes. The air stank of fire, damp, and ash. It seemed that the city had taken as much as it could take—but the Germans were saving the worst for last.

The Blitz reached its peak of terror on May 10, 1941. The Luftwaffe flew more than 500 flights over London that night. Once again, fires raged throughout the city. Once again, thousands of homes and other buildings were destroyed. Once again, the people of London suffered the loss of wives, husbands, parents, children and friends. More than 1,400 Londoners were killed on that one night, and thousands more were injured. At least 12,000 were left homeless. It was one of the most horrible nights of a horrible war. But—although no one in London knew it yet—that night would mark the end of the Blitz.

There would be many more air raids on London. Death and devastation would often rain down from the skies. But the continual heavy bombing known as the Blitz came to an end with the raid of May 10. The Germans had decided it was not worth it. They were losing too many planes needed elsewhere, and they were getting nothing in return. They had hoped to break the spirit of the people of London, but they had failed.

The Battle of Britain—the Battle of London, really—was Hitler's first defeat, and it was, as it turned out, a vital one. If Hitler had conquered England, he would have been unchallenged in Europe. He and his allies would have had a stranglehold on what were left of the free nations of the world, including the United States. He had almost gotten it. If the Luftwaffe had kept up its assault on the RAF, Britain's air defenses would have been destroyed. By switching their attacks to London and the other cities, the Germans gave the RAF the chance to recover. In doing so, they lost all chance to invade England.

Without London's sacrifices, England would have lost the Battle of Britain and Hitler might have won the war. Instead, London became a symbol of hope: the center of resistance to Hitler and the Nazis. The city filled with exiles from the conquered nations of Europe. It was from London that the French General, Charles De-Gaulle, kept alive the dream of a free France. And it was in London that the supreme allied commander, General Dwight D. Eisenhower, had his headquarters while the Allies planned the D-Day invasion that would eventually free Europe from the Nazis.

A family sits amid their possessions after their home was destroyed by a bomb.

★ ★ ★ ★ ★ ★ ★ ★ ★ ★

6

GETTING ON
WITH IT

"At first, it was very frightening," Jane Hartwright says today. "We felt like sitting targets." As time went on, however, people learned to live with the dangers, and even the horrors, of war. "You got immune to people dying. You got up, and there was rubble, and somebody else's house had gone, and another family had been killed, and you just got on with it."[1]

★ ★ ★

In the first days of the Blitz, almost everyone rushed to the nearest shelter whenever a siren went off. Some parents even sent their children to the shelters between bombings, to save room for the family when the bombing resumed. "When things were at their worst," remembers Sister Anna, an Anglican nun who was then a young woman, "people went from shelter to work to shelter, and hardly got into the fresh air at all."[2]

People brought books with them to the shelters. Many wom-

Sleeping in an underground shelter

en brought their knitting. When they were done with their family's garments, they knitted sweaters for British sailors. Those children whose schools were open brought their homework. A few even smuggled in their pets.

Being in a shelter was no guarantee of safety, however. Many suburban Londoners were killed in the small shelters they had constructed in their backyards. At least one whole family was found dead in their shelter with no apparent wounds. A nearby bomb had sucked all the oxygen out of their lungs.

Even the big shelters were not immune. The shelter in the crypt of the Church of the Holy Redeemer, in Chelsea, suffered a direct hit on September 14, 1940. When rescue workers arrived, they had to remove a woman's body from the entrance in order to get inside. A survivor described the scene inside: "Bodies, limbs, blood, and flesh mingled with little hats, shoes, and all the small necessities which people took to the shelters with them.... People were literally blown to pieces and the mess was appalling."[3] Another bomb smashed into a shelter containing 160 people.

After a while, some Londoners stopped going to the shelters. The Germans might kill them, but they couldn't control their lives. Thousands of people even refused to take cover in their homes until bombs were actually falling nearby. Only one of the people in Sister Anna's street regularly rushed to the shelter whenever the sirens sounded, and she was the only one who was killed—struck down by a bomb on her way to the shelter.[4]

★ ★ ★

While most people dreaded the bombings, some seemed to relish the danger, the intensity, and even the sheer destructiveness of them. Among those attracted by the danger was Winston Churchill, who would sometimes go up to the roof of the prime minister's residence to witness an attack himself.

Even those less foolhardy acknowledge, in Jane Hartwright's words, that "there was a certain excitement in living on the edge."[5] There was also a certain beauty. The writer Evelyn Waugh described the London sky looking "as though a thousand tropic suns were simultaneously setting."[6] Many who stayed underground while the bombs were falling rushed outside afterward to take in the terrible raging beauty of the fires.

Londoners took great satisfaction from surviving the attacks and going on about their business. "In the mornings, sitting in the buses," writes Sister Anna, "there was such a sense of surprised relief to be still alive. People would talk as though they'd known each other all their lives.... The attitude was that Hitler would never break us down—the worse things got, the more determined people were....."[7]

"Indeed," Churchill would later write, "many persons seemed envious of London's distinction, and quite a number came up from the country in order to spend a night or two in town, share the task, and see the fun."[8]

To the annoyance of most young people, school attendance was required during most of the war. The upper-class boys returned to the relative safety of their expensive public schools outside London, and continued their educations uninterrupted. The children who remained in London, meanwhile, had to face both the regimented drudgery of their classes and the dangers of bombing raids.

Since children could not be sent home during a raid, German attacks sometimes prolonged the school day. Whenever a raid occurred, the children were instructed to shove their books into their desks and file out of the classroom and down to the assigned shelter. Once there, they sat side by side on the floor, or on wooden benches, and waited for the bombing to end.

After school, many children were left to their own devices. For some, the rubble of bombed-out buildings became their playgrounds. They were a perfect setting for war games, and a treasure trove for scavenging. Pieces of shrapnel (fragments of exploded bombs) or bits of downed planes were all greatly prized.

A German bomb put a crater in this backyard garden.

While some children continued to run wild throughout the war, others became more responsible. The strong had to look out for the weak. Older children had to take care of their younger brothers and sisters, since it often fell to them to see the young ones through the air raids.

Some children even had to look out for their own parents. "My mother was fear-ridden," Jane Hartwright, who was a young teenager at the time, explains. "I can remember having to be very tough and brave for her, and burying my fear. She didn't ask me to. But one has this thing about one's own mother."[9] She resented the fact that her father was away from home so much, leaving them to face the bombs alone. She understood that he was doing important work, acting as a fire-spotter. But she resented it anyway.

Despite the horrors all around them, Londoners still found ways to enjoy themselves. Many theaters and other public entertainment spots closed briefly early in the war, but most soon reopened. Before long, Londoners were going out—to movies, restaurants, pubs, nightclubs, and live theaters—almost as often as before the war.

Of all the entertainments, movies were the most popular with children and young adults. Patriotic action movies in which heroic Britishers defeated evil Nazis were among the most popular of all. Even Sherlock Holmes—in the form of Basil Rathbone—was enlisted in the war against Germany.

Families entertained themselves in their homes, gathering around the piano, playing, singing, and dancing together. Often, neighbors were invited to join in for an impromptu party.

The older teenagers congregated in dance clubs, which were also frequented by servicemen on leave. For those wanting to relieve their wartime tensions, the jitterbug was all the rage. Those in a more romantic mood danced cheek to cheek to sentimental wartime ballads like "There'll Come Another Day," "He Wears a Pair of Silver Wings," and the ever popular "White Cliffs of Dover." It was at these dance clubs that many London women met the British, Canadian, Australian, and American men who would become their husbands.

Servicemen enjoy a break from the war at a dance club.

A sitting room has a new view after a bomb raid.

People got used to doing less. England had to be supplied by sea, and the Germans were doing their best to stop ships from reaching port. Most of what did get through was needed for the war. Many common products, from toys to furniture, disappeared from the stores early in the war. Leather was so scarce that some children were given wooden shoes to wear.

All vital materials were rationed, including petrol (as the British call gasoline), rubber, steel, and food. Especially food. Rich or poor, everyone was given ration coupons. They were good for specific amounts of food each week. Each adult, for example, was allowed two ounces of tuna and one egg a week. Once your coupons were used up, it didn't matter how much money you had, you couldn't get any more.

Even after a bombing raid, displaced Londoners wait to enjoy afternoon tea.

Some foods couldn't be found at all. Many young people had to wait till the war was over before they got their first taste of a banana or a peach. Later in the war, American military rations began to appear, thanks to the American soldiers passing through London. Canned beef stew was very popular, although one girl remembers it as having an "awful lot of peas" in it.

Rationing was hard on those who were used to eating a lot, but it made things better for those who were used to less. Because butter was rationed equally, for instance, some poor families got to taste it for the first time.

All fuels were rationed. Since most Londoners relied on coal for heat, coal rationing produced great suffering. Two very harsh winters occurred during the war, and several people were frozen to death in their own homes for lack of coal.

Gasoline rationing made car travel difficult, so almost everyone got bicycles. There always seemed to be long queues (or lines) at the bus stops and, because of shortages, in the stores as well. Britons got so used to standing in lines that even today they are famous for the patience with which they "queue up" to wait for things.

Since almost everything was strictly rationed, there was a lot of black-market activity. A farmer who brought a few extra eggs into town might swap them for a tankful of gasoline. Ann Ackermann remembers getting an extra orange from a softhearted grocer. "That was strictly against the rules," she explains, "but he liked little girls."[10]

Not all the black marketing was so harmless. Criminals stole large amounts of rationed items and sold them to the highest bidder. All this made the shortages worse for everyone else.

Everyone was expected to help the war effort, and most Londoners did so eagerly. People with big yards planted victory gardens. Everything they could raise, from tomatoes to radishes, was badly needed to reduce the food shortages. Most school classes had their own gardens, and the students spent part of each school day tending them. The food they grew was used in the school's own kitchen. Tens of thousands of city children also spent summer vacations at harvest camps, where they helped to gather the crops that fed the country.

People of all social classes and ages did volunteer work when their regular work was done. Even those who didn't have to work

A Victory Garden in a bomb crater

for a living lent a hand. The Duchess of Kent rolled bandages for wounded soldiers. The king's brothers knitted sweaters for the navy. Tens of thousands of women joined groups like the Women's Auxiliary Volunteer Service, or the Red Cross nursing service known as the Voluntary Aid Detachment.

Some volunteers explored the wreckage of bombed buildings, searching for survivors. A few were known as "body sniffers" because they had the ability to smell a body buried under a pile of rubble. It was said that the best of them could actually smell whether the unseen body was alive or dead. Others had the grisly job of matching up the pieces of bodies shattered by the bombs. They did the best they could, but sometimes the various arms, legs, and other body parts just wouldn't match up. It is likely that parts of several bodies were sometimes buried together as one.

Both men and women did duty as air-raid wardens. They patrolled the neighborhoods, made sure that people followed the blackout rules, and helped people get to and from the air-raid shelters. There were even special "animal guards," who came out after every raid to care for wounded animals.

Men who were too old for the regular military volunteered for the citizens' army known as the Home Guard. Doctors, plumbers, lawyers, laborers, tavern keepers, and bookkeepers drilled shoulder to shoulder, practicing to defend the country if the German invasion ever came. Even women took part in such activities. Some girls as young as seventeen took lessons in firing machine guns.

The Boy Scouts and Girl Guides (the British version of the Girl Scouts) were enlisted to help. Older boys were recruited to join the Air Training Corps, Army Cadets, or Sea Cadets, newly created organizations that pretrained them for duty in the real thing. Simi-

A butler from the Royal Palace turns over metal kitchenware to be used in the war effort.

lar groups were formed to train young girls.

Even younger children helped by taking part in government-run salvage drives. They turned the talents they had developed scavenging for souvenirs in bombed-out buildings to finding scrap materials that could be recycled for the war effort.

★ ★ ★

One pleasant summer evening in 1944, Jane Hartwright was returning home from a date. As she and her companion were strolling through some trees, they heard an odd noise coming from the sky, like the throbbing engine of a small plane in trouble. Suddenly, the noise abruptly stopped. Looking off in that direction, they saw a trail of orange streaking down through the darkness. Seconds later, there was the sound of an explosion.

What they had seen and heard was a new kind of pilotless missile the Germans were hurling at London from a launching pad on the French coast. Called the V-1, the missile was set to travel a certain distance before its engine cut out and it dropped from the sky, exploding like a bomb when it hit the ground. The first V-1 had landed in the outskirts of London on June 13, beginning what became known as the "Little Blitz."

Londoners called the new weapons "doodlebugs," because of the insect-like sound they made. They were harder to defend against than bombers. They came in all kinds of weather, even when planes could not fly, and traveled so fast (372 miles an hour) that they were hard to hit with antiaircraft fire. Altogether, more than 2,400 V-1s hit London that summer, killing 6,000 people and injuring 18,000 more.

In September, the V-1 was replaced by an even more terrifying weapon—the much bigger, faster, and more powerful V-2. Unlike the V-1, the V-2 made no sound at all. And, traveling at 3,600

miles an hour, the V-2 was not just difficult, but impossible, to shoot down.

Workers remove an unexploded bomb

One V-2 landed near Jane Hartwright's home. The force of the explosion shattered the windows and blew the solid oak front door into fragments. Looking out at the back of the house, the

A worker at an ammunition factory sends a special gift to Adolf Hitler.

Hartwrights discovered a huge bomb crater 100 feet wide and 50 feet deep. Three children were picking themselves up from the very edge of the huge crater. The rocket had exploded right next to them, but miraculously they had not been hurt. The force of the explosion had gone down and up, passing right over their heads.

Thousands of others were not so lucky. More than 2,700 people were killed by the more than 500 V-2s that fell on London before the attacks ended in March 1945.

The V-1s and V-2s were horrifying and destructive, but they did nothing to help the German cause. In fact, they hurt it. The Allies had already launched their invasion of Nazi Europe a week before the first V-1 fell on London. The Allied forces desperately needed the military supplies being shipped to them from England. But instead of directing their rockets against Britain's ports, the Nazis had sent them against England's cities.

By launching the Blitz, Hitler had ended his chance of invading England. Now, by launching the Little Blitz, he had destroyed all hope of interfering with the Allies' march to Berlin. Through their suffering and sacrifice, the people of London had twice helped Britain to survive and win the war.

Londoners celebrate the end of the war.

★★★★★★★★★★

7

THE AFTERMATH OF WAR

The Germans surrendered on May 7, 1945. As usual, Londoners heard the news over their radios. The news had been expected, but everyone rushed to tell their neighbors. "The war is over. The war is over!" The next day was proclaimed a holiday—VE Day—Victory in Europe Day.

It seemed that all the worst days of the war had been bright and sunny. Now VE Day dawned dark and drizzly. But nobody cared. Throughout the war, the people of London had entertained themselves at impromptu parties in their homes. Now they threw an enormous party in the streets. People flocked into the public squares. One large crowd paid tribute to Churchill. Another swarmed over the huge stone lions that crouch in Trafalgar Square.

The rebuilding of London begins.

Later in the day, the sun came out, as all over the city, strangers hugged and kissed each other. There was dancing in the streets. London was safe at last!

By the next day, the mood of celebration was already dimming. The war was over, but Londoners knew the effects of the war would go on.

The city had been decimated. Virtually every historic landmark in London had been ripped by bombs or gutted by fire. Even Buckingham Palace had been hit seven times. Tens of thousands of stores, offices, factories, and other buildings had disappeared. Whole blocks had turned to rubble. Over a million homes had been either damaged or totally destroyed. Whole neighborhoods had been demolished, leaving the people who had lived there homeless. It would be many years before the city would be fully rebuilt.

★ ★ ★

Twenty thousand Londoners had died in the bombing and rocket attacks. Probably twice that many had been seriously injured, among them thousands of children. Some would never recover. They would live out their lives without their legs or their arms, their sight, or their hearing. They would grow to adulthood horribly scarred or paralyzed.

Other children would carry their wounds inside. They had seen too much. Thousands would have terrible nightmares for years. A loud noise or the smell of smoke would send them into panic. In their whole lives, many would never really feel safe again. Even those who had not been obviously unnerved would suffer long-lasting effects.

Many years after the war, Jane Hartwright would attend an air show in Vancouver, Canada, halfway around the world from London. She was a grown woman by then, and Canada was at peace. And yet, when the planes swooped down to make a pass over the crowd, Jane astonished herself and her Canadian friends by throwing herself onto the ground. It was an automatic response, an old fear that took her unawares.

It wasn't just individuals who suffered. Families were shattered. Hundreds of thousands of London's children would grow up without fathers or mothers because of the war.

★ ★ ★

The war had lasted six years. That time had consumed the childhoods of hundreds of thousands of Londoners. Boys who hadn't yet reached their teens on September 7, 1940 were flying fighters for the RAF by VE Day. Girls who had been playing with dolls during the Blitz were cuddling real babies by the time the war was over.

Looking back on it now, many of those people feel that the war cheated them out of their childhoods. This is especially true of those who lost their parents to the war. But not everyone feels that way. "I can't say I felt robbed," says Jane Hartwright. In some ways, "I gained more than I lost."[1] Ann Ackermann agrees. "I think it gave us fortitude," she says. "It probably made us tougher."[2]

They, and all the others like them, needed all the toughness and fortitude they had. The years that followed the war were hard times in England. The war had destroyed the British economy. Although everyone was overjoyed to welcome their fathers, brothers, and sisters home, the flood of returning veterans swamped the job market. Unemployment and poverty reached new levels. Shortages of housing, food, and consumer goods got worse instead of better. Rationing went on for nearly a decade after the war was over, longer than in defeated Germany!

There was social and political turmoil too. Workers who had suffered patriotically throughout the war years now struck for de-

The devastated area around St. Paul's

cent pay. Winston Churchill, who had led the country through its long crisis, was turned out of office. And, to make matters worse, the winters that followed the war were the coldest on record.

★ ★ ★

For good and bad, the war helped overturn many of the realities Londoners had always accepted as inevitable. For one thing, London would no longer be the heart of the British Empire. There would be no British Empire left. Within a few years of the war's end, almost all of Britain's remaining colonies would achieve independence. In the eyes of many Britons, it was just as well. Britain was tired.

What is more, the bombs that fell on London had blasted cracks in the walls that divided Britain's social classes. Rich and poor had faced the challenge of the war together. People of every class had served in the military, done volunteer work, and lived with the same threat of death dropping from the air. German bombs didn't care whether they landed in the poverty-stricken East End or in elegant Mayfair. The V-rockets didn't care what social class their victims belonged to.

Many upper-class Britons came out of the war with a new respect for the people of the lower classes. They realized, as Labor Minister Ernest Bevin once said, that "If a [lower class] boy can save us in a Spitfire, the same brain can be turned to produce a new world."[3] The walls between the classes were not totally demolished by the war, but they were weakened. Great holes were beginning to appear.

After the war, there were new efforts to provide for the welfare of the poor. Among them were measures to grant free education to the children of the lower classes. Those efforts eventually paid off. When England finally returned to prosperity in the late 1950s, the working class would have a bigger share in that prosperity than ever before. And, when there was a great burst of creative energy in England in the 1960s, it would be led by writers and artists from the working class. Most of them had been children during the war.

The last word on the men, women, and children of London belongs to their king. Throughout the war, King George VI was a living symbol of London's will to survive. Even during the worst days of the Blitz, he stayed in the city, determined to share the dangers and sorrows of his people.

The king made a practice of visiting neighborhoods hard hit by German bombs. Walking through the wreckage of the bombed-out buildings, he gave comfort to the people who had lived in them and let them know he felt their loss.

One neighborhood man was so moved that he could not contain himself. "You're a great king!" he cried out.

"You're a great people!" the king replied.[4]

King George VI and Queen Elizabeth visit a bombed neighborhood.

SOURCE NOTES

★ ★ ★

CHAPTER ONE

1. Peter Ustinov, *Dear Me* (Boston: Little, Brown, and Co., 1977), 61.

CHAPTER TWO

1. *Reader's Digest Illustrated History of World War II* (London: Reader's Digest, 1989), 19.
2. Ibid., 25.
3. "Ultimate Issue," *Time*, September 11, 1939, 26.

CHAPTER THREE

1. "Foreign News," *Time*, October 9, 1939, 22.
2. John Cabot, "Town and Country Face to Face," *Commonweal*, November 24, 1939, 10.
3. Angus Calder, *The People's War: Britain—1939-1945* (New York: Pantheon, 1969), 44.
4. Ibid., 41.
5. "Christmas," *Time*, December 25, 1939, 14.

CHAPTER FOUR

1. *Reader's Digest Illustrated History*, 34.
2. Ibid., 34.
3. James C. Humes, *Winston Churchill: Speaker of the Century* (New York: Stein and Day, 1980), 186-187.
4. Ibid., 189.

1. Conversation with Jane Hartwright, April 7, 1991.
2. Ibid.
3. Conversation with Ann Ackermann, April 9, 1991.
4. "First Major Casualty," *Time*, March 18, 1940, 45.
5. Ibid.
6. *Newsweek*, November 18, 1940, 30.
7. *Reader's Digest Illustrated History*, 52.
8. Winston Churchill, *Their Finest Hour* (Boston: Houghton Mifflin, 1949), 370-371.

CHAPTER FIVE

1. Conversation with Jane Hartwright, April 7, 1991.
2. Letter from Sister Anna, of Langan College, Belfast, April 8, 1991.
3. Francis Faviell, "The Blitz: Chelsea, 14 September 1940," in John Carey, ed. *Eyewitness to History* (New York: Avon, 1987), 539.
4. Letter from Sister Anna, April 8, 1991.
5. Conversation with Jane Hartwright, April 7, 1991.
6. Calder, *The People's War*, 170.
7. Letter from Sister Anna, April 8, 1991.
8. Churchill, *Their Finest Hour*, 372.
9. Conversation with Jane Hartwright, April 7, 1991.
10. Conversation with Ann Ackermann, April 9, 1991.

CHAPTER SIX

1. Conversation with Jane Hartwright, April 7, 1991.
2. Conversation with Ann Ackermann, April 9, 1991.
3. *Newsweek*, October 1940, 24.
4. *Time*, September 23, 1940, 32.

CHAPTER SEVEN

FURTHER READING

✦ ✦ ✦

BOOKS

Calder, Angus. *The People's War: Britain—1939-1945.* New York: Pantheon, 1969.

Calder, Ritchie. *The Lesson of London.* London: Secker and Warburg, 1941.

———. *Carry on London.* London: English University Press, 1941.

Churchill, Winston. *Their Finest Hour.* Boston: Houghton Mifflin, 1949.

Fitzgibbons, Constantine. *Blitz.* London: Wingate, 1957.

Ingersoll, Ralph. *Report on England.* New York: Simon and Schuster, 1940.

Marchant, Hilde. *Women and Children Last.* London: Gollancz, 1941.

Mosley, Leonard, ed. *Battle of Britain.* Alexandria, Virginia: Time-Life, 1977.

Murrow, Edward R. *This Is London.* New York: Simon and Schuster, 1941.

Turner, Ernest Sackville. *The Phoney War on the Home Front.* London: M. Joseph, 1940.

PERIODICALS

Readers interested in the general subject of London during the war might also consult virtually any issue of the leading newsmagazines of the period, most notably *Time* and *Newsweek*, both of which ran regular reports on events in the city.

FILMS

Perhaps the best child's-eye view of life in London during World War II in any medium is the 1987 movie *Hope and Glory,* written, produced, and directed by John Boorman, who was himself a child in the city during the Blitz.

INDEX

✹ ✹ ✹